THE TWELVE DAYS OF WINTER

A School Counting Book

by Deborah Lee Rose
illustrated by Carey Armstrong-Ellis

ABRAMS BOOKS FOR YOUNG READERS
NEW YORK

1
On the first day of winter,
my teacher gave to me . . .

Winter
Fun!

. . . a bird feeder in a snowy tree.

Winter Fun!
Hibernation Zone

2 On the second day of winter,
my teacher gave to me
TWO teddy bears
and a bird feeder in a snowy tree.

ANTARCTIC
ANIMALS

3

On the third day of winter,
my teacher gave to me
THREE penguins,
two teddy bears,
and a bird feeder in a snowy tree.

4

On the fourth day of winter,
my teacher gave to me
FOUR weather words,
three penguins,
two teddy bears,
and a bird feeder in
a snowy tree.

Field Guide to Birds
Reminder:
Tomorrow evening-
Skating party!

5

On the fifth day of winter,
my teacher gave to me
FIVE gold stars,
four weather words,
three penguins,
two teddy bears,
and a bird feeder in a snowy tree.

6 On the sixth day of winter,
my teacher gave to me
SIX socks for stuffing,
five gold stars,
four weather words,
three penguins,
two teddy bears,
and a bird feeder in a snowy tree.

CONTAINS
of
FLUFF!
80 lbs.

7

On the seventh day of winter,
my teacher gave to me
SEVEN flakes for snipping,
six socks for stuffing,
five gold stars,
four weather words,
three penguins,
two teddy bears,
and a bird feeder in a snowy tree.

2 + 1 = 3

8

On the eighth day of winter,
my teacher gave to me
EIGHT bells for jingling,
seven flakes for snipping,
six socks for stuffing,
five gold stars,
four weather words,
three penguins,
two teddy bears,
and a bird feeder in a snowy tree.

Gg Hh
Mm
Rr Ss

9

On the ninth day of winter,
my teacher gave to me
NINE worms for watching,
eight bells for jingling,
seven flakes for snipping,
six socks for stuffing,
five gold stars,
four weather words,
three penguins,
two teddy bears,
and a bird feeder in
a snowy tree.

10

On the tenth day of winter,
my teacher gave to me
TEN holes for stitching,
nine worms for watching,
eight bells for jingling,
seven flakes for snipping,
six socks for stuffing,
five gold stars,
four weather words,
three penguins,
two teddy bears,
and a bird feeder in
a snowy tree.

snow
snowman
snowball
snowflake
snowstorm
snow peas

11

On the eleventh day of winter,
my teacher gave to me
ELEVEN cubes for gluing,
ten holes for stitching,
nine worms for watching,
eight bells for jingling,
seven flakes for snipping,
six socks for stuffing,
five gold stars,
four weather words,
three penguins,
two teddy bears,
and a bird feeder in
a snowy tree.

SUGAR CUBES
Gloppy Glue

12

On the twelfth day of winter,
my teacher gave to me
TWELVE treats for tasting,
eleven cubes for gluing,
ten holes for stitching,
nine worms for watching,
eight bells for jingling,
seven flakes for snipping,
six socks for stuffing . . .

Weekly Weather
Monday
snowy
sleet
miserable
Tuesday
windy
slushy
cabin fever
Wednesday
sunny
freezing rain
Thursday
cloudy
hail
Friday
icy
blizzard
SOS
REX

. . . five gold stars,
four weather words,
three penguins,
two teddy bears . . .

Winter
sleet
snowy

. . . and a bird feeder
in a snowy tree.

For all my school experts, big and small, and for Carey,
whose drawings made me want to see more of these characters' adventures —D. L. R.

To the co-op teachers at Coastal Ridge Elementary School —C. A-E.

Designed by Celina Carvalho
Production Manager: Alexis Mentor

Library of Congress Cataloging-in-Publication Data
Rose, Deborah Lee.
The twelve days of winter : a school counting book / by Deborah Lee
Rose ; illustrated by Carey Armstrong-Ellis.
p. cm.
Summary: A cumulative counting verse in which a child lists items
pertaining to winter given by the teacher, from twelve treats for tasting to one bird feeder in a snowy tree.
[1. Winter—Fiction. 2. Counting.] I. Armstrong-Ellis, Carey, ill.
II. Title.
PZ7.R7149Twe 2006
[E]—dc22
2005011580

Published in 2006 by Abrams Books for Young Readers, an imprint of Harry N. Abrams, Incorporated, New York.

Printed and bound in China
10 9 8 7 6 5 4 3 2 1

115 West 18th Street
New York, NY 10011
www.abramsbooks.com

LAKE COUNTY PUBLIC LIBRARY
3 3113 02573 3314